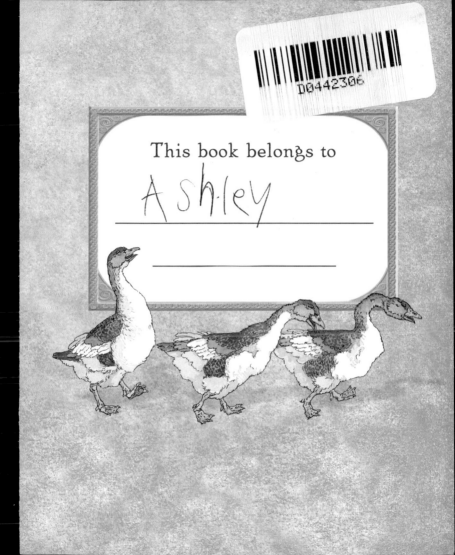

This book belongs to

Ashley

Jack and Jill

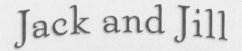

Mother Goose *for* Boys and Girls

Jack and Jill went up the hill
To fetch a pail of water.
Jack fell down
and broke his crown,
And Jill came tumbling after.

Little Bo-peep
   has lost her sheep,
And can't tell where
   to find them.
Leave them alone,
   and they'll come home,
And bring their tails
   behind them.

Little Boy Blue,
   come blow your horn.
The sheep's in the meadow,
   the cow's in the corn.
What! Is this the way
   you mind your sheep,
Under the haystack
   fast asleep?

Polly, put the kettle on,

Polly, put the kettle on,

Polly, put the kettle on,

We'll all have tea.

Sukey, take it off again,

Sukey, take it off again,

Sukey, take it off again,

They're all gone away.

About the bush, Willie,
about the bee-hive,
About the bush, Willie,
I'll meet thee alive.

Handy Pandy,
Jack-a-dandy,
Loves plum cake
and sugar candy.
He bought some at
a grocer's shop,
And out he came,
hop, hop, hop!

Little Miss Muffet
  Sat on a tuffet,
Eating some curds and whey.
  There came a great spider
  That sat down beside her,
And frightened Miss Muffet away.

Little Jack Horner
Sat in a corner,
Eating a Christmas pie.
He put in his thumb,
And pulled out a plum,
And said: "Oh, what a
good boy am I!"

Mary, Mary,
quite contrary,
How does your
garden grow?
With silver bells
and cockleshells
And pretty maids
all in a row.

Tom, Tom, the piper's son,
Stole a pig, and away he run.
The pig was eat,
And Tom was beat,
And Tom ran crying
down the street.

Georgy Porgy,
    pudding and pie,
Kissed the girls
    and made them cry.
When the boys
    came out to play,
Georgy Porgy
    ran away.

Lucy Locket lost her pocket;

Kitty Fisher found it.

There was not a penny in it,

But a ribbon round it.